A. Mary F. (Agnes Mary Frances) Robinson

The New Arcadia

And Other poems

A. Mary F. (Agnes Mary Frances) Robinson

The New Arcadia
And Other poems

ISBN/EAN: 9783744770477

Printed in Europe, USA, Canada, Australia, Japan

Cover: Foto ©Andreas Hilbeck / pixelio.de

More available books at **www.hansebooks.com**

THE NEW ARCADIA

AND OTHER POEMS

BY

A. MARY F. ROBINSON

AUTHOR OF "EMILY BRONTE"

" Their lives, a general mist of error "

WEBSTER

BOSTON
ROBERTS BROTHERS
1884

University Press:

JOHN WILSON AND SON, CAMBRIDGE.

TO

VERNON LEE.

PROLOGUE

THE NEW ARCADIA.

PROLOGUE.

Not only in great cities dwells great crime;
Not where they clash ashore, and break and moan,
Are waters deadliest; and not in rhyme,
Nor ever in words, the deepest heart is shown.
But, lost in silence, fearful things are known
To lonely souls, dumb passions, shoreless seas,
And he who fights with Death may shrink from these.

Alas! not all the greenness of the leaves,
Not all their delicate tremble in the air,
Can pluck one stab from a fierce heart that grieves.
The harvest-moon slants on as sordid care
As wears its heart out under attic eaves,
And though all round those folded mountains sleep,
Think you that sin and heart-break are less deep?

You see the shepherd and his flocks a-field,
Hunger and passion are present there, no less.
Fearful! when suddenly starts forth revealed
Man's soul, unneighbored in its hideousness,
Man's darker soul, a memory to possess
Henceforth, by which all nature pales and dies,
As a city suddenly wan under sunset skies.

And I have heard long since, and I have seen,
Wrong that has sunk like iron into my soul,
That has eaten into my heart, has burned me and been
A pang and pity past my own control,
And I have wept to think what such things mean,
And I have said I will not weep alone,
Others shall sorrow and know as I have known.

Others shall learn and shudder, and sorrow, and know
What shame is in the world they will not see.
They cover it up with leaves, they make a show
Of Maypole garlands over, but there shall be

A *wind* to scatter their gauds, and a wind to blow
And purify the hidden dreaded thing
Festering underneath ; and so I sing.

If God had given a sword into my hand
I would go forth and fight the battles of God ;
If God had given me wisdom, I would stand
And summon up truth with my divining rod :
But I have only a song at my command,
The froth of the world a song, as water weak :
Yet since it is my weapon, let me speak.

And listen you that are more mighty than I,
Who can go forth and do what I but dream --
Bear with me if I am vain, bear patiently.
I have lived so long with shadows, who only seem,
That now these real men murdered make me cry,
As there were none on earth but I and they,
And all else echoes, phantoms, witches' play.

But this is real, that men are wild, and hard,
And villanous; while other men look on
And say, it is not so: a smell of nard
And not of blood is here; not woebegone
These faces, but content. Ah, what reward
For all our strife had we their quiet homes
And quiet hearts and wish that never roams!

So say ye; for to think in all the world
There is so still and sweet a resting-place,
Where never the angry seas of passion are hurled
Against necessity, where none is base
And none is starved. There is a sort of grace
To keep so sweet a vision in your eyes,
And as you smile the true thing starves and dies.

Oh, help! help! it is Murder that I cry,
And not a song to sell. Now if you smile
And hear me you are mad; you are mad, or I.
For I do not sing to enchant you or beguile;

I sing to make you think enchantment vile,

I sing to wring your hearts and make you know

What shame there is in the world, what wrongs, what
    woe ;

Because your deaf ears, only, are to blame,

Not your deaf hearts. Look now, and if you see

Men as they are, contented in their shame,

I know that you will help, you will let them be

Foreseeing, noble, wise, and even as ye ; —

Only your eyes I ask, only your ears,

The rest I leave to him who sees and hears.

Then let me sing, and listen to my song,

Though it is rough with sobs, and harsh and wild,

And often wanders, and is often long,

As mothers tell the death-bed of their child.

My child was gentle visions, and all were wrong,

And false, and cruel ; and I bury it here :

Lend me your spades, — I do not ask a tear.

Lend me your souls, and do not stand aloof,
Saying what happy lives these peasants win,
Praising the plushy lichens on the roof.
Leave off your praising, brothers, and come in.
See, round the hearth, squat Ignorance, Fever, Sin.
See on the straw the starving baby cries ;
The mother thanks her God another dies.

Ah, look within !   Without, the world is fair,
And you are all in love with solitude ;
Yet look within : Evil and Pain are there.
Look, ye who say Life best is understood
Where greenish light falls dappling the moss-floored wood,
Look at the dumb brute souls who suffer and strive ; —
Leave the dead world, and make their souls alive !

THE NEW ARCADIA.

I.

THE HAND-BELL RINGERS.

THE HAND-BELL RINGERS.

I.

LAST night the ringers came over the moor
    To ring us in Christmas-tide ;
They entered in at our garden door :
We sat and watched the yule logs roar,
    They stood on the grass outside.

We sat within in the warmth and light,
    The fire leapt red and blue ;
Each frosted lamp was a moon of white
The growing plants half hid from sight,
    Letting the radiance through.

And the white and the red lights filled the room,
    And flickered on bracket and ledge,

On the pale sweet pinks and the cactus bloom,
With its crimson flush, and the leafy gloom
    Of the sill's geranium-hedge.

We sat, making merry, shut in from the rain
    And the Christmas cold outside.
But hark ! the carol goes pealing again ;
The ringers are out in the cold, 't is plain,
    Ringing in Christmas-tide.

II.

I left the fire with its flicker and roar,
    And drew the curtains back.
On the edge of the grass stood the ringers four,
With the dim white railing behind, and the moor
    A waste of endless black,

With, somewhere burning, aloof, afar,
    A single lonely light ;

But never a glimmer of moon or star
To show where the unseen heavens are
    Through the whole dark width of the night.

In front of the rail, in a shadowy row,
    Stood the ringers, dim and brown ;
Their faces burned with a faded glow,
And spots of light now high, now low,
    With the bells leapt up and down.

At first, a faint red blur in the night
    Is a face — no more than that ;
And merely a shifting disk of light
Each great bright bell, to the dazzled sight
    Worth scarce the looking at.

Till slowly the figure, barely guessed,
    Grows human ; the face grows clear :
The tall, red prophet who leads the rest,
The sallow lad with the hollow chest,
    You see them all appear.

You catch the way they look and stand,
    The listening clench of the eyes ;
The great round hand-bells, golden and grand,
Grasped a couple in either hand,
    And the arms that fall and rise.

III.

So much I behold, and would never complain,
    As much and no more could I see.
As clear as air is the window pane
'Twixt me in the light and them in the rain,
    Yet strange they look to me !

Grim, solemn figures, all in a row,
    Intent on the carol they ring ;
But I see no less in the pane the glow
Of the cactus-crimson, and to and fro
    The flames their flicker fling.

My ribbon breast-knot dances across
  The leader's solemn brow,
The moon-globed lamps burn low in the moss,
And my own pale face, as it seems, they toss,
  With the ringing hand-bells now.

So dark is the night, so dark, alas !
  I look on the world, no doubt ;
Yet I see no less in the window-glass,
The room within, than the trees and grass,
  And men I would study without.

MAN AND WIFE.

MAN AND WIFE.

THE bracken withers day by day,
   The furze is out of bloom.
Over the common the heather is gray,
   And there's no gold left on the broom ;
And the least wind flutters a golden fleck
From the three tall aspens that grow in the beck.

Yet, oh, I shall miss it to-morrow night,
   The wild, rough sea of furze ;
And the cows coming down, looking large and white,
   And the tink of each bell as it stirs,
The aspens brushing the tender sky,
And the whirr of the geese as they homeward fly.

'T is the first grief ever I owned to mind
  Until to-night, good neighbor ;
For I could work when John went blind,
  And I never dreaded labor ;
And Willie grew so good a son,
We never fretted, I and John.

Ah, me !   We 've waited here at the gate
  Many and many an even,
When Willie lingered a little late,
  And I 've thought it seemed like Heaven,
To stand, the work all done, and look
At the yellow and pink of the sky in the brook.

And John, I know, though he 's blind as a stone,
  And bent with a life of pain,
He 'll miss it sore when he sits alone,
  And wish he could see it again —
As though it were Heaven itself.   Ah, me !
There 's only clouds that the blind can see.

No doubt there was trouble enough in the past,

    But trouble we bore together;

And trouble shared is no worse to last

    Than the bite of wind or weather:

But now we 're old to begin anew —

To suffer apart — oh, it 's hard to do!

It 's not the shame that I dread, you see,

    Though it 's sharp; nor the workhouse fare;

Oh, any place is the same to me,

    Could we stay together there:

But John 's stone-blind — my John, my man —

I 'd like to serve him while I can.

But he 'll be apart in one long room,

    And I as strange in another;

At the end of the day I 'll sit down in the gloom,

    And be no man's wife or mother;

And I 'll miss his voice and the tap of his stick

Till my throat grows choked and my sight grows thick.

I 'll not be dull?   There are people enough
    In the House?   Is that what you say?
Yes, every one there that I do not love,
    And only my man away :
Voices and steps coming in and out,
But never the one that I care about.

I 'd rather starve in the snow with John !
    But that would be wicked, I know ;
Indeed, we might live with our only son,
    And never stir out in the snow.
But burden his back with our useless lives,
And palsy the arm that struggles and strives.

Nay, Will has another to think of — my Will,
    'T is time the lad was wed ;
He 's waited long, and he would wait still,
    Till John and I were dead :
But better the Poorhouse, better far,
Than only to live as a fret and a bar.

Ah, **we** remember, I and John,

The waiting till youth is spoiled ;

I 'd never owe **my** bread **to a son,**

And sit while he toiled and moiled,

And see the lass he hoped to wive

Grow old unmarried, since I was alive.

That was the way in our time, though,

But I never liked the way !

It kept us single till forty, I know,

And married us old and gray ;

And set me only one child on **my knee ;**

Who shall not suffer **as much** from me.

And so to-morrow we **leave the place**

To go to the House up yon ;

Yes, as you say, **'t is a** sad disgrace ;

Yet we 've worked hard — I and **John —**

We 've worked until we **can work no more,**

And all our labor **has left us poor.**

Oh, never I thought it would come to this
   When we loved each other first ;
And yet, had I seen with the first, first kiss,
   I know I 'd have faced the worst :
I 'd live the same life over again —
Hardship and all — so I 'll not complain.

Neighbor, I 'm not unthankful ; indeed,
   I know they are good to the poor
Who take us away from our cold and need,
   When we 're grown too old to endure :
Only I think they can have no heart,
For all their kindness, to house us apart.

III.

THE SCAPE-GOAT.

THE SCAPE-GOAT.

SHE lived in the hovel alone, the beautiful child.
  Alas, that it should have been so !
But her father died of the drink, and the sons went wild ;
  And where was the girl to go?

Her brothers left her alone in the lonely hut.
  Ah, it was dreary at night
When the wind whistled right through the door that
        never would shut,
  And sent her sobbing with fright.

She never had slept alone ; for the stifling room
  Held her, brothers, father — all.
Ah, better their violence, better their threats, than the gloom
  That now hung close as a pall !

When the hard day's washing was done, it was sweeter
    to stand
  Hearkening praises and vows,
To feel her cold fingers kept warm in a sheltering hand,
  Than crouch in the desolate house.

Ah, me ! she was only a child ; and yet so aware
  Of the shame which follows on sin.
A poor, lost, terrified child ! she stept in the snare,
  Knowing the toils she was in.

Yet, now, when I watch her pass with a heavy reel,
  Shouting her villanous song,
Is it only pity or shame, do you think, that I feel
  For the infinite sorrow and wrong?

With a sick, strange wonder I ask, Who shall answer
    the sin,
  Thou, lover, brothers of thine?
Or he who left standing thy hovel to perish in?
  Or I, who gave no sign?

IV.

JANET FISHER.

3

JANET FISHER.

PART I.

WHERE Janet Fisher lived and died,
   The Eastland marshes reach away
For miles on miles of either side
A river desolately wide
   That is itself as drear as they.

With tufts of purple marish flowers
   The rough gray grass is islanded ;
The travelling thunder broods for hours
In gathered purple, where there lowers
   The frequent tempest overhead.

Immense the eternal arch of sky ;
   Immense — utterly barren, too —

The plain in which no mountains lie
To mar that vastness, bounded by
  The far horizon's shadowy blue.

Only the river's gradual bend
  Shows stunted willows set in rows,
Rank pasture, kine the children tend,
Blown curls of smoke that swerve and ascend
  From leaning hovels clustered close.

For on this barren, aguish swamp,
  Even here is life, even here are men
To shake with palsy, stiffen with cramp,
To die ere fifty of the damp
  And fetid vapors of the fen.

Though how a village came to grow
  In such a vile and deathly air
None knows ; it may be long ago
The outcasts of some crime or woe,
  Fleeing for refuge, sheltered there ;

And through the habit of their race,
  Or fearing yet the wrath of men,
Their children settled in the place,
And reaped scant harvest, in the face
  Of death, upon the poisonous fen.

And since the end was always near,
  And life so hard ; and since they knew,
Save sloth and lust, no joys ; each year
They served their senses less in fear,
  And more like beasts and viler grew.

Few friends were there, tho' all were kin :
  There was much strife, and many raids ;
The hovels that they huddled in
Housed men whose brutal love was sin,
  Nameless children, and shameless maids.

Even among this soulless herd
  Lived Janet Fisher ; but she went

Along their streets, and no man stirred
Her quiet heart with look or word
   To harm the village Innocent.

They meant she was an idiot born,
   This one fair sight in foulest place ;
This girl as fresh as early morn ;
So fair — and yet too sad to scorn ;
   Too sunk for any hind to embrace.

Their one fair thing, their one thing good,
   And she bereft of sense or will,
So mere a mask of womanhood —
Sad ; — but there was no heart to brood
   Upon the irremediable ill.

Yet crazy Janet found them kind —
   They took her when her mother died
To live in turn with each ; to wind
Their well-ropes, bind their sheaves, and mind
   Their cattle grazing far and wide.

But often by the river-brim
  She strayed, scattering seeds and flowers,
To wade in clear green shallows, and swim
Against the stream ; or, through the dim
  And quiet twilight, row for hours.

Day long, night long, her spirit slept,
  And nothing shook the sullen drowse ;
Yet oft a shadowy pleasure crept
All through her, where the boats were kept,
  Beneath the dangling willow boughs.

She was so strong, she liked to feel
  Her rapid stroke lend wings to the boat ;
The water dashing against the keel ;
The wind in her face and hair ; the teal
  And plovers crying, the weeds afloat.

Then only she — who was so far
  Behind the merest child of all —

Was prouder, stronger, than others are ;
And she could row to the harbor bar
  And back, ten miles, ere night dews fall.

PART II.

But all the harvest long, forlorn,
  Unloosed, the boat rocked to and fro,
While Janet slept from eve till morn,
Dead-tired with gathering in the corn
  From daybreak till the light was low.

How glad she was when autumn whirled
  The slender yellowing willow leaves,
When all the plants looked shrivelled and curled,
And no more corn or fruit in the world
  Was left to gather under eaves.

For then one evening, when the plain
  Was strangely bright i' the sun, and black
With thunder and unfallen rain
The sky, she sought her boat again,
  And bent the yielding branches back —

The thinning willow boughs — and found
  A man, half-stripped, beside the boat,
Burying hurriedly underground
And heaping yellow leaves around
  A stained and faded soldier's coat.

She stood behind him, nothing loth
  To watch his work unseen a span,
For she was neither scared nor wroth ;
The splendor of the scarlet cloth
  Engrossed her, not the haggard man.

" Give me it ! " eager Janet said
  At last ; the man who heard her shook

Alarmed, and turned his startled head.
He was as wan and gray as the dead,
   And even Janet feared his look.

"All 's up," he moaned. "Ay, call them out!
   I 'm spent, you 're strong," he moaned; — "hit hard,
I 'm down. Don't stare so, woman; shout!
Why, don't you know what you 're about?
   I 'm a deserter — there's reward.

"I 'm spent." But towards the scarlet coat
   He saw unheeding Janet go;
Then turned, and turning, saw the boat.
"Oh, God!" he cried, with straining throat,
   "Girl, will you help me?" "I can row."

Poor Janet! — all those prayers were vain
   To reach the incommunicable
Dim soul in her; and yet 't was plain
He wished her, prayed her, to remain —
   And one thing only she could do well.

She smiled.   Her masters on the fen
　Bade her : Do this, bear such a load,
Go there — for they were brutish men.
But this man spake her fair ; and then
　She longed to show him how well she rowed !

Within the boat she took her stand ;
　He followed her unquestioningly,
Got in, sat down, at her command ;
She pushed the boat off from the land,
　And, with the current, sought the sea.

Fierce yellow sunlight, beetling clouds
　Heaped up in blackness overhead ;
Still air, in which the beasts were cowed,
And all the sounds were over-loud —
　Yet Janet felt no thrill of dread.

Inland the sea-mews fled, that know
　The earliest tempest-mutterings ;

The swallows, skimming very low,
Dipped, and a livid western glow
  Glanced off their sheeny underwings.

On through the ominous dusk the bark
  That knew no fear, that had no soul,
Made for the sea.   How should it hark
The wind, or see the air grow dark,
  Or feel the widening waters roll?

And soulless as itself, and rash,
  Janet rowed on, elate and proud;
And thankful to escape the lash,
Her fellow heard no waters dash,
  And did not see the gathering cloud.

Speechless he drowsed for many a mile,
  Sunk to inert fatigue, half dead;
At last : " It takes a long, long while,"
He muttered.   Janet turned — her smile
  Filled all his veins with sudden dread.

He started, shook the torpid drowse
  Off him like water ; all around
The river heaved in waves ; and soughs
And moans of wind began to arouse
  The storm ; he could not see the ground.

Black walls of stormy air shut in
  The boat ; above, a gloomy vault
Shattered by lightning ; roar and din
Where sea and hurtling stream begin
  Their desperate, endless rebuff and assault.

"Woman !" he shouted ; " mad-woman, speak ! —
  Why did you let me sleep so long?
Is it the sea, the sea, you seek ? "
The tears fell into the spray on her cheek :
  " Help me," she wailed ; " I 'm spent, you 're strong."

His words ! his prayer ! No safety, then,
  If she were mad ; no means to avert

The end.　Far backwards lay the fen,
And here, instead of a world of men,
　　A danger no man shall desert.

Had she gone mad, perhaps, from fright,
　　This woman?　" Oh, my God ! " he cried ;
" To be alone at sea, by night ;
Lost in a storm — no hope, no light,
　　A maniac for my only guide ! "

She crouched upon the lowest plank
　　And cried, and dashed her hands in the wave
That drenched her dress, and made so lank
And straight her hair — that slowly sank
　　Them down towards the engulfing grave.

The man stooped down and looked at her,
　　Half-blind with swirling spray of the sea.
Horror, impotent wrath, despair
At heart.　What did she say?　A prayer?
　　" Poor crazy Janet ; pity me ! "

Then was he lost in very truth —
How wild his hope ! how vain his trust !
This woman — this, his angel of ruth —
Had lured him to his death ; in sooth,
To kill her would be merely just.

Should he kill her?   Sea and sky,
In answering storms, heaved up, hung down ;
They seemed to touch, they met so nigh.
One moment more all else must die :
Why should he kill her?   Let her drown !

" Help me !" she shrieked.   But who could swim
In such a sea, — a toppling bank
Of waves?   She sprang, and clung to him ;
Then noise, hate, storm, death, all grew dim ;
He caught her — tried to save her — sank.

But when the storm was stilled at last,
The fishers found him on the strand,

One arm stretched out, still battling past
The waves, it seemed, and clasping fast
    A woman's corpse with one stiff hand.

They knew him not, but her they knew ;
    Poor Janet, missed a day and night.
Then, wind-uncovered, stained with dew,
They found the coat ; the wonder grew,
    And the sad story came to light.

V.

THE ROTHERS.

4

THE ROTHERS.

As far as you can see, the moor
 Spreads on and on for many a mile,
And hill and dale are covered o'er
 With many a fragrant splash and isle
Of vivid heather, purple still,
Though the bracken is yellow on dingle and hill.

The heather bells are stiff and dry,
 Yet honey is sweet in the inmost cell ;
The bracken 's withered that stands so high,
 But sleeping cattle love it well. —
Thorny fern and honeyless heather,
A friend who chills with the blighting weather.

A mile towards the western sun
 The Rothers have their wooded park;
Never another so fair an one
 Sees from his poise the singing lark.
When Rother of Rother first began
Recks not the memory of man.

It stands there still, a red old house,
 Rother, set round with branchy pines;
The heather is red beneath the boughs,
 And red are the trunks where the slant sun shines,
And the earth is ruddy on hollow and height:
But the blood of a Rother's heart is white.

Right royal faces, none the less,
 And gracious ways when the world is kind;
But trust a Rother in your distress, —
 A hollow hemlock stem you find,
Where you looked for a sapling to cling to and save
You yet from the chasm below like a grave.

And now they are ended — the faithless race ;

  Sir Thomas was never a Rother born,

He took the name when he took the place,

  With the childless wife whom he laughs to scorn :

And his life is a cruel and evil life —

But let none pity his craven wife.

She — oh marvel of wonder and awe —

  O angered patience of God ! — I say

God sees our sins ; for a sign I saw

  Set in the western skies one day —

White, over Rother, white and pale

For many a mile over hill and dale.

Now let me make the marvel clear.

  When Edward, last of the Rothers, died

He left two orphan daughters here :

  Little children who scarce could ride,

Clutching the mane with baby hands,

O'er half an acre of their lands.

I think I see the sorrel mare,
   Staid, old ; and, tumbled on her neck,
Flushed faces, dimpled arms, and hair
   Of crimpy flax with a golden fleck ;
As by the side, with timid graces,
Well to the fore, the prim nurse paces.

A pretty cavalcade !   Ah well,
   The Rothers ever loved a horse !
And so one day Sir Edward fell,
   Out hunting ; dragged along the gorse
For yards, one foot in the stirrups still,
The hunters found him upon the hill.

They brought him home as cold as stone,
   Into his house they bore him in ;
Nor at his burial any one
   Was there to mourn him, of his kin,
Save those two babies, grave and grand
In black, who could not understand.

Poor wondering children, clad in crape,
 Who knew not what they had to mourn,
Careful their sash should keep its shape
 That papa, when he should return,
Might praise each little stiff new gown —
All day they never would sit down.

Poor, childish mutes, they stood all day
 With outspread skirts and outspread hair,
And baby lips, less pink than gray
 (So pale they were), and solemn stare ;
They watched our mourning, pained and dumb,
Wondering when papa would come,

And give them each a ride on his horse,
 And toss them both in the air, and say
"A Rother is sure in the saddle, of course,
 But never a Rother rode better than they,"
And send them up to bed at last
To sleep till morning, sound and fast.

At last each whitish-flaxen head
   Drooped heavily, each baby-cheek
Its pallid shadow-roses shed —
   The straight black legs grew soft and weak —
Father and frocks alike forgot
They fell asleep, and sorrowed not.

Yet pitiable they were, alone
   They were, twin heiresses of five,
With lands and houses of their own,
   And never a friend in the world alive
Save one old great-aunt, over in France,
Who knew them not, nor cared, perchance.

We little fancied she would come —
   Quit palms, and sun, and table d'hôte
For two unknown little girls at home ;
   But soon there came a scented note
With half the phrases underscored,
And French at every second word.

And soon she followed, — she would sigh,
  And clasp her hands, and swear " by God ; "
Her black wig ever slipped awry,
  And quavered with a trembling nod ;
Her face was powdered very white,
Her black eyes danced under brows of night.

Such paint ! Yet were I ever to feel
  Utterly lost, no saint I 'd pray,
But, crooked of ringlets and high of heel,
  I 'd call to the rescue old Miss May ;
No haloed angel sweet and slender,
Were half so kind, so stanch, so tender.

She loved the children well, but most
  The girl who least was like herself —
Maudie, at worst a plaintive ghost,
  Maudie, at best a laughing elf,
With eyes deep flowering under dew,
Such tender looks of lazy blue.

Florence was stronger, commonplace
  Perhaps, but good, sincere, and kind.
There was no Rother in her face,
  There was no Rother I could find
In her heart either; but who knows?
My son shall not marry a daughter of Flo's.

You see I hate the Rothers, I!
  Unjust, perhaps, all are not vile
It may be — but I cannot try,
  When I think of a Rother now, to smile.
You hate the Irish, perhaps? the Turks?
In every heart some hatred lurks.

But these two girls I never hated,
  I thought them better than their race;
Who would not think a curse out-dated
  When from so fresh and young a face
The Rother eyes looked frankly out,
The Rother smile flashed no Rother's doubt?

Well, they were young, and wealthy, and fair ;

    It seemed not long since they were born,

When Florence married Lawrence Dare,

    Then Maud, alas ! Sir Thomas Thorn,

A bitter, dark, bad, cruel man

Sir Thomas, now, of the Rother clan.

For now we come to the very root

    Of the passionate rancor I keep at heart

Flowering in words, but the bitter fruit

    Is still unripe for its sterner part.

Well, Maud, too, married, Miss May was free

To go wherever she wished to be.

Homeless, after so many years

    Of sacrifice ! Where could she go?

But she, she smiled, choked back her tears,

    " Of course," she said, " it must be so, —

So kind, her girls, to let her come

Three months to each in her married home ! "

And first at Rother with the Thorns
   In her old home she stayed a guest;
   .   .   .   .   .
But must I think of all the scorns
   That made your age a bitter jest, —
Whose memory like a star appears
Thro' the violent dark of that House of tears?

Your Maud was changed; — a craven slave
   To her unloving husband now;
The bitter words she could not brave,
   The silent hatred of eyes and brow
Estranged her not; and oh, 't is true !
To gain his favor she slighted you.

And yet you stayed !   And yet you stayed —
   Hoping to win your dear one back —
Thinking through pain, not sin, she strayed
   From the old, good, well-known heavenly track.
Alas, your lamb had gone too far — .
Farther from you than the farthest star.
   .   .   .   .   .

At last the three months ended ; then
  I heard Miss May was very ill ;
It was the first of autumn when
  Our roads are bad, so I chose the hill
And the brow of the moor, as I rode away
To Rother, where my good friend lay.

And now for my sunset. Is 't not strange
  That heaven, which sees a million woes
Unmoved, should pale, and faint, and change
  At one more murder that it knows?
And yet I think I could declare
A horror in that sunset's glare.

As I was riding over the moor
  My back was turned to the blazing white
Of the western sun, but all around
  The country caught the strange bright light ;
The tufts of trees were yellow, not green ;
Gray shadows hung like nets between.

Such yellow colors on bush and tree !
　　Such sharp-cut shade and light I saw !
The white gates white as a star may be :
　　But every scarlet hip and haw,
Border of poppies, roof of red,
Had lost its color, wan and dead !

So strange the east, that soon I turned
　　To watch the shining west appear.
Under a billow of smoke there burned
　　A belt of blinding silver, sheer
White length of light, wherefrom there shone
A round, white, dazzling, rayless sun.

There, mirror-like it hung and blazed,
　　And all the earth below was strange,
And all the scene whereon I gazed
　　Even to the view-line's uttermost range
Hill, steeple, moor, all near and far
Was flat as shifting side-scenes are.

Lifeless, a country in the moon
It seemed, that white and vague expanse,
So substanceless and thin, that soon
I fell to wonder, by some chance
Of a sketcher's fancy — how would fare
The tones of flesh in that strange white glare?

A freak of the painter's cautious eye
Which notes all possible effect —
I scarcely daub, but I love to try, —
So, full of the whim, I recollect,
I stretched my own right arm and gazed
At the hand, quite black where the full light blazed.

That was too near, I smiled and turned,
And shook the reins and rode away,
And looked where the eastern forest burned
With its golden oaks. But who were they
In the dog-cart, there, just under the trees?
They should prove my fancy ! A grip of the knees,

And I reached them ; why, the Thorns they were,
  The Thorns livid, and clear, and plain
In the ugly light, nor could I dare
  To ask if my friend were at ease or in pain ;
So bitter-sour looked Maudie's mouth —
The whole face dried like grass in a drouth.

But what was that, see, pent like a calf
  That the butcher drives to the slaughter-house,
Tied in the back of his cart, and half
  Already slain with the jolt of his brows
On the planks of the side — oh, what was that
Laid there, like death, laid prone and flat?

What was that burden prone and weak —
  What was it, lying there behind
Formless, helpless?   I could not speak,
  Nor in their eyes an answer find ;
I stopped them, looked again, and saw —
Oh, is there, then, on earth no law,

No thunder in heaven?   On the floor
 It was, indeed, an old gray head
That jerked from side to side ; no more,
 Only an old, gray woman dead
Behind there, in the jolting cart,
And a woman in front with a devil's heart.

True, that indeed they did not know
 Miss May was dead, I grant ; enough,
They thought her merely dying, and though
 The air was cold, the road was rough,
Could say " Her three months' stay is o'er,
She is our promised guest no more.

" Now let her go to Florence Dare ;
 No need for us to nurse her, now ;
The drive will do her good, the air
 Strike freshly on her fevered brow,
And in the cart warm shawls are spread " —
Where, as you know, I found her dead.

Because they cast her away, my friend,
　　Because her nursling murdered her.
There, my long story has an end
　　At last.　I leave you to infer
The moral old enough to be true :
" Do good, and it is done to you."

But bid me not forgive and forget ;
　　Forget my friend, forget a crime
Because the county neighbors fret
　　That I 'll not meet at dinner-time
Ingratitude and murder?　Nay,
Touch pitch and be defiled, I say.

VI.

COTTAR'S GIRL.

COTTAR'S GIRL.

THE lilac boughs at Cottar's farm
   Were sprouting into spikes of red,
The April sun was scarcely warm
   When first of all I heard it said
   That Cottar's girl was ill or dead.

There was no other doctor near
   For many miles, so I set out,
Wondering I was left to hear;
   They had not sent; sudden, no doubt.
   Poor child, to die when lilacs sprout.

     .

Sixteen years old, poor Cecily!
   I never thought her very strong.

And yet the very soul of glee,
  Always ready with laugh and song;
  Such vivid natures last not long.

Over merry, the least surprise
  Would turn her pale and like to faint;
Slender, with such thin hands, and eyes
  Too bright; the sort of girl to paint,
  But not to marry; a hectic saint.

Hysteric to the last degree;
  But yet there was no cause for death,
No cause in that, poor Cecily.
  She was her parents' very breath,
  Their only child, love, hope, and faith.

She was so different from them,
  The stern, decorous, formal pair;
To see her stitching at her hem,
  Or spelling out the Sunday prayer,
  Was youth and laughter in the air.

They chided her and said her name
  Was one that sober yeomen bore ;
She laughed ; they loved her all the same,
    Perhaps they loved her all the more ;
    No Cottar was so gay before.

Ah, well, they 'll miss her ! There the house,
  Severely white, stood fronting me.
I passed beneath the lilac boughs,
    The palest buds were gone. Ah me,
    I thought, they 're plucked for Cecily.

Perhaps it was the heavy day,
  Perhaps because she was sixteen ;
But, for some cause I cannot say,
    I missed the girl, who had not been
    My friend, among the tender green.

I now recall how long I knocked
  Before the mother raised the latch, —

The mother, with her smile that mocked,
  The sinuous brows that did not match,
  And eyes that always seemed to watch.

Not then she smiled ; " She 's gone," she said.
  " My Cecily 's gone ; she died last night.
She went to sleep and she was dead.
  No pain."   She stared like one at bay ;
  And then she asked me would I say

The cause of death ; and I was glad
  In all that gloom to be of aid.
I stepped within the chamber sad,
  Where, stiff beneath the white, was laid
  The shrouded body of the maid.

And by his little daughter's bier
  The farmer, huddled in his coat,
Looked heavier for his grief and fear,
  As I have seen a stranded boat
  Look larger than it did afloat.

A little while we did not speak,
  I stood beside the hallowed bed,
And looked at Cecily ; her cheek
  Was rounded still, was scarcely dead.
  " What did she die of ? " then I said.

None spoke. I saw the mother glance
  Sharp at the hulking, silent man,
Who did not speak and looked askance.
  And as I waited for a span
  The dead girl grew more drawn and wan.

At last I raised my voice again,
  And then, " She choked," the mother said,
" But yet I think she felt no pain."
  'T was then I saw above the bed
  A jug half filled with shotted lead.

At first I merely saw ; I swear
  It was the mother's eyes, not mine,

That made me as I looked at her
  Perceive, or rather half divine,
  Why that jar was an evil sign.

And, swift as sight, the whole grew plain.
  I knew that I had heard or read
A village nostrum, cruel, vain,
  That dosed poor choking girls with lead,
  To sink the ball i' the throat, it said.

A vile fantastic remedy,
  Ignorant poison.   Oh, I thought
I could have fairly raged to see
  The farmer grown quite old, distraught,
  And Cecily dead — and all for naught.

I took the jar, " But how," I cried,
  " Could such a deed be done by you ! "

The woman looked at me and sighed:
  " I was her mother, sir ; I knew
There was no other thing to do."

Old Cottar gave nor sign nor word,
  And when I made him understand
He shifted not his head nor stirred,
  But muttered feebly in his hand :
  " She minds the house, and I the land."

There was no getting at the truth ;
  Besides, I think he did not know :
They would not kill their child forsooth !
  It seemed a hopeless tangle, so
  I rose at length and meant to go.

But, as I turned, the mother came,
  Asked me to write a pack of lies,
To sign the death with some forged name ;
  And something in that woman's eyes
  Filled me with horrible surmise.

I stooped above their daughter dear,
  Not yet disgraceful, only dead.
Beneath the lilacs on the bier,
  Crushed in the corpse, an unborn dread
  Weighed heavier than their murderous lead.

VII.

THE WISE-WOMAN.

THE WISE-WOMAN.

In the last low cottage in Blackthorn Lane
    The Wise-woman lives alone ;
The broken thatch lets in the rain,
And the glass is shattered in every pane
    With stones the boys have thrown.

For who would not throw stones at a witch,
    Take any safe revenge
For the father's lameness, the mother's stitch,
The sheep that died on its back in a ditch,
    And the mildewed corn in the grange?

Only be sure to be out of sight
    Of the witch's baleful eye !

So the stones, for the most, are thrown at night,
Then a scuffle of feet, a hurry of fright —
    How fast those urchins fly !

And a shattered glass is gaping sore
    In the ragged window frame,
Or a horseshoe nailed against the door,
Whereunder the witch should pass no more,
    Where sayings and doings the same.

The witch's garden is run to weeds,
    Never a phlox or a rose,
But infamous growths her brewing needs,
Or slimy mosses the rank soil breeds,
    Or tares such as no man sows.

This is the house.   Lift up the latch —
    Faugh, the smoke and the smell !
A broken bench, some rags that catch
The drip of the rain from the broken thatch —
    Are these the wages of Hell ?

Is it for this she earns the fear
  And the shuddering hate of her kind?
To moulder and ache in the hovel here,
With the horror of death ever brooding near,
  And the terror of what is behind?

The witch — who wonders? — is bent with cramp,
  Satan himself cannot cure her,
For the beaten floor is oozing damp,
And the moon, through the roof, might serve for a lamp,
  Only a rushlight's surer.

And here some night she will die alone,
  When the cramp clutches tight at her heart.
Let her cry in her anguish, and sob, and moan,
The tenderest woman the village has known
  Would shudder — but keep apart.

Should she die in her bed! A likelier chance
  Were the dog's death, drowned in the pond.

6

The witch when she passes it looks askance :
They ducked her once, when the horse bit Nance ;
    She remembers, and looks beyond.

For then she had perished in very truth,
    But the Squire's son, home from college,
Rushed to the rescue, himself forsooth
Plunged after the witch. — Yes, I like the youth
    For all his new-fangled knowledge.

How he stormed at the cowards !   What a rage
    Heroic flashed in his eyes !
But many a struggle and many an age
Must pass ere the same broad heritage
    Be given the fools and the wise.

" Cowards ! " he cried.   He was lord of the land,
    He was mighty to them, and rich.
They let him rant ; but on either hand
They shrank from the devil's unseen brand
    On the sallow face of the witch.

They let him rant ; but deep in each heart
  Each thought of some thing of his own
Wounded or hurt by the Wise-woman's art ;
Some friend estranged, or some lover apart.
  Each heart grew cold as stone.

And the Heir spoke on, in his eager youth,
  His blue eyes full of flame ;
And he held the witch, as he spoke of the Truth ;
And the dead, cold Past ; and of Love and of Ruth —
  But their hearts were still the same.

Till at last — "For the sake of Christ who died,
  Mother, forgive them," he said.
"Come, let us kneel, let us pray !" he cried.
But horror-stricken, aghast, from his side
  The witch broke loose and fled !

Fled right fast from the brave amends
  He would make her then and there,

From the chance that heaven so seldom sends
To turn our bitterest foes to friends, —
    Fled at the name of a prayer.

Poor lad, he stared so ; amazed and grieved.
    He had argued nearly an hour ;
And yet the beldam herself believed,
No less than the villagers she deceived,
    In her own unholy power !

Though surely a witch should know very well
    'T is the lie for which she will burn.
She surely has learned that the deepest spell
Her art includes could never compel
    A quart of cream to turn.

And why, knowing this, should one sell one's soul
    To gain such a life as hers, —

The life of the bat and the burrowing mole, —
To gain no vision and no control,
  Not even the power to curse?

"T is strange, and a riddle still in my mind
  To-day as well as then.
There 's never an answer I could find
Unless — O folly of humankind!
  O vanity born with men!

Rather it may be than merely remain
  A woman poor and old,
No longer like to be courted again
For the sallow face deep lined with pain,
  Or the heart grown sad and cold.

Such bitter souls may there be, I think,
  So craving the power that slips,
Rather than lose it, they would drink
The waters of Hell, and lie at the brink
  Of the grave, with eager lips.

Who sooner would, than slip from sight,
    Meet every eye askance ;
Whom threatened murder can scarce affright ;
Who sooner would live as a plague and a blight
    Than just be forgotten ; perchance.

VIII.

MEN AND MONKEYS.

MEN AND MONKEYS.

THE hawthorn lane was full of flower ;
　On the white hedge the apple-trees
　Sent down with every gust of breeze
A light, loose-petalled blossom-shower.

The wide green edges of the lane
　Were filmed with faint valerian ; white
　Archangels tall, the bees' delight,
Sprang lustier for the morning's rain.

The scent of May was heavy-sweet ;
　The noon poured down upon the land,
　The nightingales on either hand
Called, and were silent in the heat.

For even in the distant deep
  Green-lighted forest glades, the noon
  Grown heavy with excess of boon,
Weighed all the sultry earth to sleep.

The herds, the flowers, the nightingales
  All drowsed ; and I upon the edge
  Of grass beneath the flowering hedge
Lay dreaming of its shoots and trails.

When, starting at the sound of feet,
  I saw the Italian vagrants pass ;
  The monkey, man, and peasant lass,
Who figure on our village street

At race-time in the spring ; nor song,
  Caper, nor hurdy-gurdy tune
  Seemed left in them this blazing noon
As wearily they trudged along,

Their sallow faces drawn, their eyes
   Fixed on the miles of dust that went
   Before them, their round shoulders bent
Beneath a load of vanities.

The man tramped first, upon his back
   The hurdy-gurdy, with an ape
   Who strained his lean and eager shape
Towards the woman's gayer pack

Of rags and ribbons.   What a sight
   Among the blossoms and the green !
   I think there never can have been
A stranger shadow in the light.

They did not pause to look upon
   The apple-blossom and the may ;
   They only saw the dust that they
Raised in their dismal trudging on.

They did not even stop to hear
    The rare sweet call of the nightingale ;
    The hurdy-gurdy's squeak and yell
Was too accustomed in their ear.

I watched them plod their stolid way
    Still on ; but suddenly I heard
    The monkey mimic the singing-bird,
And snatch a trail of the flowering may.

And down the road I saw him still
    Catching and clutching the blossom white,
    And waving his long, black arms in delight,
Until they passed over the brow of the hill.

IX.

CHURCH-GOING TIM.

CHURCH-GOING TIM.

Tim Black is bedridden, you say?
  Well now, I'm sorry. Poor old Tim!
There's not in all the place to-day
  A soul as will not pity him.

These twenty years, come hail, come snow,
  Come winter cold, or summer heat,
Week after week to church he'ld go
  On them two hobbling sticks for feet.

These years he's gone on crutches. Yet
  One never heard the least complaint.
And see how other men will fret
  At nothing ; Tim was quite a saint.

And now there 's service every day,
　　I say they keep it up for him ;
We busier ones, we keep away —
　　There 's mostly no one there but Tim.

Yes, quite a saint he was.　Although
　　He never was a likely man
At his own trade ; indeed, I know
　　Many 's the day I 've pitied Nan.

She had a time of it, his wife,
　　With all those children and no wage,
As like as not, from Tim.　The life
　　She led !　She looked three times her age.

The half he had he 'ld give to tramps
　　If they were hungry, or it was cold —
Pampering up them idle scamps,
　　While Nan grew lean and pinched and old.

He 'ld let her grumble.   Not a word
   Or blow from him she ever had —
And yet I 've heard her sigh, and heard
   Her say she wished as he was bad.

Atop of all the fever came ;
   And Tim went hobbling past on sticks.
Still one felt happier, all the same,
   When he 'ld gone by to church at six.

Not that I wished to go.   Not I !
   With Joe so wild, and all those boys —
It takes my day to clean, and try
   To settle down the dust and noise.

But still — out of it all, to glance
   And see Tim hobbling by so calm,
As though he heard the angels' chants
   And saw their branching crowns of palm.

7

And when he smiled, he had a look,
   One's burden seemed to loose and roll
Like Christian's in the picture-book :
   It was a comfort, on the whole.

It made one easier-like, somehow —
   It made one, somehow, feel so sure,
That far above the dust and row
   The glory of God does still endure.

You say he 's well, though he can't stir :
   I 'm sure you mean it kind — But, see,
It 's not for him I 'm crying, sir,
   It 's not for Tim, sir ; it 's for me.

X.

THE SCHOOL CHILDREN.

THE SCHOOL CHILDREN.

THESE at least are clean and fresh,
  All I wished to see !
Hair a flaxen flossy mesh,
  Waving loose and free
Round their ruddy English flesh.

Now at last they 're out of school,
  Happy, happy time !
Now a truce to book and rule,
  Task in prose or rhyme,
Thought of prize or dunce's stool.

How they laugh and run about !
  What if now and then

Somewhat overloud a shout
   Reach you busier men ;
Could the children play without ?

What, you call them rude and rough,
   Overprone to strife ?
Still I find them good enough
   For such eager life ;
What should they be thinking of ?

Though they know a mint of things,
   So their mothers say,
Read and write, and rattle strings
   And strings of dates away,
Bible judges, English kings,

I, for one, should never dare
   Such a gage to fate,
As to stand with any there
   Pouring name and date,
Faster, faster . . . . O despair !

That one passed in Euclid, look !
   This can draw and sing !
And the girls, I think, can cook
   Any mortal thing :
So they quote their cookery-book.

Ah — you cry — too much they know
   For their lowlier rank ;
Teach them but to plant and hoe,
   But to beg and thank,
For the clown needs keeping low.

Nay, but listen, neighbor, pray —
   Once a Flemish seer,
David Joris, so they say,
   Saw in trance appear
Kings and knights in great array.

Through his twilit painting-room
   Stalk the sombre host,

Priests and prelates grandly loom —
   Every one a ghost,
Silent as the silent gloom.

Very sad and over-worn,
   Pale and very old,
Look the solemn brows that mourn
   Under crowns of gold,
Grown too heavy to be borne.

Kings and priests, and all so gray,
   All so faint and wan,
Drifting past in still array,
   Ever drifting on,
Till at length he saw them stay.

Saw a second vision rise
   Through the twilit air,
Heard what laughter and lisping cries,
   Saw what tumbled hair,
Rosy limbs and rounded eyes !

Playing children — much the same
  As we see them here,
Laughing in a merry game —
  Rose before him clear ;
But they clove the dusk like flame.

Heeding not the ghostly throng,
  David heard them sing ;
At the echo of their song
  Saw each ghostly king
Lift his eyes, look hard and long.

Till at length, as when a breeze
  Bends the rushes well,
Captains, kings, great sovereignties,
  Bent, and bowed, and fell,
Kneeling all upon their knees.

Laying at the children's feet
  Each his kingly crown,

Each, the conquering power to greet,
　Laying humbly down
Sword and sceptre, as is meet.

Then, unkinged and dispossessed,
　Rose the weary host,
Glad at last to cease and rest ;
　For to every ghost
Comes the time when peace is best.

Since our crowns must fall to them,
　When beyond our reach
Falls our dearest diadem,
　Neighbor, let us teach
Every child to prize the gem.

For, be sure, the new things grow
　As the old things fade.
As we train the children, so
　Is the future made
That shall reign when we are low.

All the work we would have wrought

    Must by them be done ;

We shall pass ; but not our thought,

    While in every one

Lives the lesson that we taught.

EPILOGUE TO THE NEW ARCADIA.

THE stunted lives from hunger never free,
 The crowded towns, the moors where never hoe
 Stirs in the fallow soil, where live and grow
The grouse and pheasant where the man should be,
The shiftless, hopeless, long, brute misery
 That gathers like a cloud, racked to and fro
 With lightning discontent — I cannot show,
I cannot say the dreadful things I see.

And worse I see, more spectral, deathlier far :
 Class set from class, each in its separate groove ;
 Straight on to death, I watch them stiffly move,
None sees the end, but each his separate star ;
Too wrapt, should any fall, to reach a hand ;
Nor, should one cry, would any understand.

POEMS.

I.

LOSS.

LOSS.

DEAD here in Florence !   Yes, she died.
The prophesying doctors lied
Who swore the South should save her life.
But no, she died, my little wife.

I brought her South ; the whole, long way
She was as curious and as gay
As a young bird that tries its wing,
And halts to look at everything.

O sudden-turning little head,
Dear eyes — dear, changing, wistful eyes —
Your love, your eager life, now lies
Under this earth of Florence, dead.

All of her dead except the Past —
The finished Past, that cannot grow —
But that, at least, will always last,
Mocking, consoling, Life-in-show.

Will that fade too?   Seven days ago
She was alive and by my side,
And yet I cannot now divide
The pallid, gasping girl who died
From her I used to love and know.

Only in moments lives the Past ;
One like a sunlit peak stands out
Above the blurring mist and doubt,
Into which all is fading fast.

All night the train has rushed through France,
I watch the shaken lamp-light dance
Over my darling's sleeping face.
And now the engine slackens pace

And staggers up the mountain side ;
And now the depths of night divide
And let a lighter darkness through,
A tangible, dim smoke of blue
That lights the world, and is not Light,
Before the dawn, beyond the night.

The vapor clings about the grass
And makes its greenness very green,
Through it the tallest pine-tops pass
Into the night, and are not seen.
A little wind begins to stir,
The haze grows colorless and bright,
Thicker and darker springs the fir,
The train swings slowly up the height,
Each mile more slowly swings the train,
Before the mountains, past the plain.

And through the light that is not day
I feel her now as there she lay

Close in my arms, and still asleep ;
Close in my arms, so dear, so dear ;
I hold her close, and warm, and near,
Who sleeps where it is cold and deep.

That is my boasted memory ;
That, — the impression of a mood,
Effects of light on grass and wood,
Such things as I shall often see.

But Her !　God, I may try in vain,
I shall not ever see her again —
She will never say one new word,
Scarce echo one I often heard.
Even in dreams she is not quite here —
Flitting, escaping still.　I fear
Her voice will go, her face be blurred
Wholly, as long year follows year.

Often enough I think I have got
The turn of her head and neck, but not

The face — never the face that speaks.
My mind goes seeking, and seeks and seeks.

Sometimes, indeed, I feel her at hand,
Sometimes feel sure she will understand,
If only I do not look or think . . . .
Out of an empty cup I drink !

.   .   .   .

Down Lung' Arno again to-day
I went alone the self-same way
I walked with her, and heard her tell
What she would do when she was well.

All else the same.   Upon the hill
White Samminiato watching still
Among its pointing cypresses.
And that long, farthest Apennine
Still lifts a dusky, reddish line
Against the blue.   How warm it is !
And every tower and every bridge

Stands crisp and sharp in the brilliant air ;
Only along the mountain ridge
And on the hill-spurs everywhere
The olives are a smoke of blue,
Until upon the topmost height
They pale into a livid white
Against the intense, clear, salient hue
Of that mid-heaven's azure light.

This, for one day, my darling knew.

We meant to rest here, passing through.
How pleased she was with everything !
But most that winter was away
So soon, and birds began to sing ;
For all the streets were full of flowers,
The sky so blue above the towers —
Just such a day as it is to-day,
When in the sun it feels like May.

So here I pace where the sun is warm,

With no light weight dragging my arm,

Here in the sun we hoped would save —

O sunny portal of the grave,

Florence, how well I know your trick !

Lay all the walls with sunshine thick

As paint ; put colors in the air,

Strange southern trees upon your slopes,

And make your streets at Christmas fair

With flourish of roses, fill with hopes

And wonder all who gaze on you,

Loveliest town earth ever knew !

Then, presto ! take them unaware

With a blast from an open grave behind —

The icy blast of the wind — a knife

Thrust in one's back to take one's life.

Oh, 't is an excellent, cunning snare,

For the flowers grow on, and do not mind

(Who sees, if the petals be thickened and pocked?)

And the olive, and cypress, and ilex grow on.

It is only the confident heart that is mocked,
It is only the delicate life that is gone !

How I hate it, all this mask !
Those beggars really seem to bask
In this mock sunshine ; even I am
Faint in it ; but it is all a sham,
It is all a pretence — it is all a lie —
Have I not seen my darling die?

Those mocking, leering, thin-faced apes,
Who twang their sharp guitars all night, .
They are quite thin, unreal shapes,
The figures of a mirage-show.
They do not really live, I know ;
But once I heard them swear and fight,
" God, the Stab-in-the-dark ! " they cried.
The mask fell off then.   Yes, she died.

TUSCAN OLIVES.

TUSCAN OLIVES.

(RISPETTI.)

I.

THE color of the olives who shall say?
  In winter on the yellow earth they 're blue,
A wind can change the green to white or gray,
  But they are olives still in every hue;
But they are olives always, green or white,
As love is love in torment or delight;
But they are olives, ruffled or at rest,
As love is always love in tears or jest.

II.

WE walked along the terraced olive-yard,
　　And talked together till we lost the way ;
We met a peasant, bent with age, and hard,
　　Bruising the grape-skins in a vase of clay ;
Bruising the grape-skins for the second wine.
We did not drink, and left him, Love of mine,
Bruising the grapes already bruised enough :
He had his meagre wine, and we our love.

III.

WE climbed one morning to the sunny height,
  Where chestnuts grow no more, and olives grow ;
Far-off the circling mountains cinder-white,
  The yellow river and the gorge below.
" Turn round," you said, O flower of Paradise ;
I did not turn, I looked upon your eyes.
" Turn round," you said, " turn round, look at the view ! "
I did not turn, my Love, I looked at you.

IV.

How hot it was !   Across the white-hot wall
  Pale olives stretch towards the blazing street ;
You broke a branch, you never spoke at all,
  But gave it me to fan with in the heat ;
You gave it me without a sign or word,
And yet, my love, I think you knew I heard.
You gave it me without a word or sign :
Under the olives first I called you mine.

V.

At Lucca, for the autumn festival,
  The streets are tulip-gay : but you and I
Forgot them, seeing over church and wall
  Guinigi's tower soar i' the black-blue sky,
A stem of delicate rose against the blue,
And on the top two lonely olives grew,
Crowning the tower, far from the hills, alone,
As on our risen love our lives are grown.

VI.

WHO would have thought we should stand again together,
Here, with the convent a frown of towers above us ;
Here, mid the sere-wooded hills and wintry weather ;
Here, where the olives bend down and seem to love us ;
Here, where the fruit-laden olives half remember
All that began in their shadow last November ;
Here, where we knew we must part, must part and sever ;
Here where we know we shall love for aye and ever ?

VII.

REACH up and pluck a branch, and give it me,
  That I may hang it in my Northern room,
That I may find it there, and wake, and see
  — Not you ! not you ! — dead leaves and wintry
    gloom.
O senseless olives, wherefore should I take
Your leaves to balm a heart that can but ache ?
Why should I take you hence, that can but show
How much is left behind ?   I do not know.

9

III.

STORNELLI AND STRAMBOTTI.

STORNELLI AND STRAMBOTTI.

FLOWER of the Vine !
  I scarcely knew or saw how Love began ;
  So mean a flower brings forth the sweetest **wine** !

          .   .   .   .   .

I said : " My love is like a basil-flower,
  And none will see it, pallid and minute,
For, **look, the roses hang from every bower,**
  The pomegranates bow down with scarlet **fruit.**"
" Upon the ledge," you said, " for every hour
  We choose not these, **we choose the** basil-root.
. The sweet of roses is too near a sour
  With every change of every mood **to suit.**"

          .   .   .   .

Flowers in the hay !

   My heart and all the fields are full of flowers ;

   So tall they grow before the mowing-day.

    .   .   .   .   .

" As beats the sea against the rocks ! " you cried,

   "Against your stubborn will my soul is hurl'd."

You meant the seeming-daunted broken tide,

   With scattered spray and shattered crests uncurl'd,

That, from the shore, we pity or deride ;

   And yet these dying waters, spent and swirl'd,

Their stony limits do themselves decide,

   And fashion to their will the unconscious world.

    .   .   .   .   .

Rose in the rain !

   We part ; I dare not look upon your tears ;

   So frail, so white ; they shatter, bruise, and stain.

IV.

LOVE AMONG THE SAINTS.

LOVE AMONG THE SAINTS.

AT Assisi in the Church
  Well I know the frescoed wall,
Colors dim, Martyrs slim,
    Saints you scarcely see at all,
Till the slanting sunbeams search
Through the church,
  Waking life where'er they fall.

Every evening wall and vault,
  Saint and city, starts and wakes,
One by one, as the sun
    Broadens through the dusk, and makes
Grays and reds and deep blue smalt
Of the vault
    Teem with Saints, and towers, and lakes.

High among them, clear to see,
  Is one stately fresco set ;
There they stand, hand in hand,
  Bride and bridegroom gravely met,
Francis and Saint Poverty.
Well I see
  All the Saints attending, yet.

Close their ranks by groom and bride ;
  Straight their faces, clear and pure ;
Pale in stain, pale and plain,
  Fall their ample robes demure.
Grave, these goodly friends beside,
Stands the bride,
  Shorn of every earthly lure.

But, when I was there to look,
  Not Saint Agnes nor Saint Clare
(Tall and faint, like a saint)
  But a naked captive there

Fast my wandering fancy took ;
Still I look,
  Vainly, for that face and hair.

For, amid the saintly light,
  From the faded fresco starts,
Fair and pale, thin and frail,
  Round his neck a **chain of** hearts,
Love himself in mazed affright,
Out of sight
  Of his altar and his darts.

Starved and naked, wan and thin,
  Beautiful in his distress,
Crouches Love, whom **above**
  All the saints in glory **bless.**
Here he may not enter in,
Cold and thin,
  Naked, with no wedding-dress.

From the altar and the shrine
  One turns round in frowning grace,
Bids the wild, naked child,
  Swiftly leave the holy place.
Not for thee the bread and wine
On the shrine,
  Starving god of alien race !

Yet, O Warder, was it wise
  Thus to spurn him?   Was it well?
Love is strong, lasting long,
  Him thou canst not bind in Hell ;
Scourge him, burn, he never dies,
Phœnix-wise
  Riseth he unconquerable.

Only martyred Love returns
  With an altered face and air ;
Not a child, sweet and mild,
  Fit for daily kiss and care,

But a spirit which aches and burns,
Swift he turns
  All your visions to despair.

Love you cannot reach or find,
  Love that aches within the soul,
Vague and faint, till the Saint
  Cries, beyond his own control,
For some answer that his blind
Soul can find
  But in its own vain diastole.

Ah, beware ! That phantom Love
  Drives to madness, and destroys.
Yet, to all Love must call,
  Only we may choose the voice.
And whate'er we are or prove,
Loathe or love,
  Hangs upon that instant's choice.

V.

JÜTZI SCHULTHEISS.

JÜTZI SCHULTHEISS.

TÖSS, 1300.

[Jützi Schultheiss, a mediæval Mystic, loses her gifts of **trance** and vision, because in a moment of anger she refuses to **pray for** some turbulent knights.]

THE gift of God was mine ; I lost
For aye the gift of Pentecost.

I never knew why God bestowed
On me the vision and the load ;
But what He wills I have no will
To question, blindly following still
The hand that even from my **birth**
Hath shown me Heaven, forbidding **Earth**.
I **was** a child when first I drew
In sight of God ; a subtle, new,

10

Faint happiness had drawn about
My soul, and shut the whole earth out.
Yet I was sick.   I lay in bed
So weak I could not lift my head —
So weak, and yet so quite at rest,
Pillowed upon my Saviour's breast
It seemed.   Then suddenly I felt
Great wings encompass me and dwelt
Silent awhile in awe and fear,
While swiftly nearer and more near
Descended God.   A stream of white
Shining, intolerable light,
Blinded my eyes and all grew dim.
Then stilled in trance I dwelt with Him
A little while in perfect peace,
Till, fold by fold, the dark withdrew,
I felt the heavenly blessing cease,
And angels swiftly bear me through
The dizzy air in lightning flight
Till here I woke, and it was night.

My mother wept beside my bed,

My brothers prayed ; for I was dead.

Then, when my soul was given back,

I cried, as wretches on the rack

Cry in the last quick wrench of pain,

And breathed, and looked, and lived again.

Ah me, what tears of joy there fell !

How they all cried, " A miracle ! "

And kissed me given back to earth,

The dearer for that second birth

To her who bore me first.   **Ah me,**

How glad we were !   Then Anthony,

My brother, spoke : " What God has given,"

He said, " Let us restore to Heaven."

And as he spoke beneath the rod

I bowed, and gave myself to God.

Not suddenly the gift returned.

Alas ! methinks too much I yearned

For the old earthly joys, **the home**

That I had left for evermore ;
The garden with its herbs, and store
Of hives filled full of honeycomb ;
The lambs and calves that chiefly were,
Of all we had, my special care ;
My brothers, too, all left behind,
All, for some other girl to find ;
And she who loves me everywhere,
My mother, whom I often kissed
In absence with vain lips that missed
My mother more than God above.
Much bound was I with earthly love.
So slight my strength, I never could
Have freed myself from servitude.
But He who loves us saw my pain,
And with one blow struck free my chain.
Weeping I knelt within the gloom
One evening in my convent room,
Trying with all my heart to pray,
And weeping that my thoughts would stray ;

When suddenly again I felt

The unearthly light and rest ; I dwelt

Rapt in mid-heaven the whole night through,

And through my cell the angels flew,

The angels sang, the angels shone.

The Saints in glory, one by one,

Floated to God ; and under Him

Circled the shining Seraphim.

Now from that day my heart was free,

And I was God's ; then gradually

The convent learned the solemn truth,

And they were glad because my youth

Was pleasing in the sight of Him

Who filled my spirit to the brim.

They wrote my visions down and made

A treasure of the words I said.

And far and wide the news was spread

That I by God was visited.

Then many sought our convent's door,

And lands and dower began to pour
With blessings on our house ; for thus
Men praised the Lord who favored us.

For seven long years the gift was mine,
I often saw the angels shine
Suddenly down the cloister's dark
Deserted length at night ; and oft
At the high mass I seemed to mark
A stranger music, high and soft,
That swam about the heavenly Cup,
And caught our ruder voices up ;
And often, nay, indeed at will,
I would lie back and let the still
Cold trance creep over me — and see
Mary and all the Saints flash by,
Till only God was left and I.

The gift of God was mine ; I lost
For aye the gift of Pentecost.

Now sometimes in the summer time
I stood beneath the orchard trees,
And in their boughs I heard the breeze
Keep on **a low** continuing rhyme,
And nothing else was heard beside
The little birds that sang and cried
Their Latin to the praise of God.
And under foot new grass **I trod,**
And overhead the light was green,
And all the boughs were starred **and gay**
With apple-blossoms in **between**
The fresh young leaves as sweet as they.
And as I looked upon the sun,
Who made these fair things every one
To sprout and sing and wax so strong,
My **whole** heart turned into a song.
" For, God," I thought, " this sun art **Thou,**
And Thou art in the orchard bough,
And in the grass whereon I tread,
And in the bird-song overhead,

And in my soul and limbs and voice,
And in my heart which must rejoice —
God ! " And my song stopped weak and dazed,
I seemed upon the very verge
Of some great brink, wherefrom amazed
My soul shrank back, lest should emerge
Thence — Nay, what then? What should I fear?
I to whom God was known and dear?

Once so possessed with God, I stood
In prayer within the orchard wood,
When some one softly called my name,
And shattered all my happy mood.
Towards me an ancient Sister came,
" Quick, Jützi, to the hall ! " she cried ;
And swiftly after her I hied,
And swiftly reached the convent hall,
Now full of struggle and loud with brawl.

Close to the door aghast I stayed,
Too much indignant and afraid

To ask who wrought this blasphemy.
Then the old nun crept nearer me,
And whispered how some knights to-day,
Riding to Zürich's tourney-fray,
Had craved our shelter and repast,
And how we made the postern fast,
Because they were so rough a crew,
Yet gave them food and rest enew
In the great barn outside the gate ;
And how they feasted long and late
Till, drunk, they stormed the postern door,
And sacked the buttery for more.
Nor this the end ; for, having done,
One shouted " Nassau ; " straightway one
" Hapsburg." The battle was begun.

She looked at me afraid and faint,
With eyes that mutely begged for aid ;
For I was safe and I a saint,
She thought, who was a frightened maid ;

And through the clamor and the din

I heard her say, " They can but sin,

Having not God within their heart ;

But we, who have the better part,

Must pray for them to Christ above,

That in the greatness of His love

He pardon them their sins to-day."

And then she turned her eyes away.

But I looked straight before me where

The unseemly blows and clamors were,

And cold my heart grew, stiff and cold,

. For I had prayed so much of old,

So vainly for these knights-at-arms,

Who filled the country with alarms —

Too often had I prayed in vain,

Too often put myself in pain

For these irreverent, brawling, rough,

And godless knights — I had prayed enough !

" Let God," I cried, " do all He please ;

I pray no more for such as these."

Then swift I turned and fled, as though
I fled from sin, and strife, and woe,
Who fled from God, and from His grace.
Nor stayed I till I reached the place
Where I had prayed an hour ago.

I stood again beneath the shade
The flowering apple-orchard made ;
The grass was still as tall and green,
And fresh as ever it had been.
I heard the little rabbits rush
As swiftly through the wood ; the thrush
Was singing still the self-same song,
Yet something there was changed and wrong.
Or through the grass or through my heart
Some deadly thing had passed athwart,
And left behind a blighting track ;
For the old peace comes never back.

God knows how I am humbled, how
There is in all the convent now

No novice half so weak and poor
In all esteem as I ; the door
I keep, and wait on passers-by,
And lead the cattle out to browse,
And wash the beggars' feet ; even I,
Who was the glory of our house.

Yet dares my soul rejoice because,
Though I have failed, though I have sinned,
Not less eternal are the laws
Of God, no less the sun and wind
Declare His glory than before,
Though I am fallen, and faint, and poor.
Nay, should I fall to very Hell,
Yet am I not so miserable
As heathen are, who know not Him,
Who makes all other glories dim.
O God, believed in still though lost,
Yet fill me with Thy Holy Ghost —
Let but the vision fill mine eye

An instant ere the tear be dry ;

Or, if Thou wilt, keep hid and far,

Yet art Thou still the secret star

To which my soul sets all her tides,

My soul that recks of nought besides.

Have not I found Thee in the fire

Of sunset's purple after-glow ?

Have not I found Thee in the throe

Of anguished hearts that bleed and tire ?

God, once so plain to see and hear,

Now never answering any tear.

O God, a guest within my house

Thou wert, my love thou wert, my spouse ;

Yet never known so well as now

When the ash whitens on my brow ;

And cinders on my head are tossed,

Because the gift I had I lost.

VI.

LAUS DEO: A.D. 1213.

GOD is the common soul of all.
The Christ Himself Who saveth me,
Nearer to God I dare not call
Than is the ruining wind at sea
Or the lost corpse whom no one weeps.
Not this nor that is God; but He
All things pervades, in all things sleeps,
And by His nature, not His will,
The round world from destruction keeps.
Not this nor that is God; and still
I know, I know He may be found
More closely than in cloud or rill:
For, lost within my soul's profound
And inner depth, a being moves
That is not me, that is not bound

11

By earthly limits, earthly **loves,**

That is **not** stirred by what **I feel,**

And which condemns not, nor approves.

Beside that inner depth I reel,

Looking therein, therefrom I shrink ;

So far the empty dark doth wheel,

So far, so wide below the brink.

And yet I know the chasm is His ;

Nor till I fall and dare not think,

But simply through the dark abyss

Keep falling down, and still to **fall,**

Shall I behold God as He is.

.   .   .   .   .

O vast abysm of God, O lone

And awful chaos unexplored,

Where buds the latest flower unknown,

Where all our undreamed deeds are stored

Unborn and still, O mighty womb,

In which the unconscious, voiceless Word

Dwells without life alive !   O tomb,

Which buries all the past **no less**

Than **us in Thine eternal room !**

O God, too far, too strange to bless

Me that would drag myself to Thee,

Take from my **soul** its separateness,

And let myself **no more be me !**

Take from me memory, thought and soul,

Drowned and confounded let **me be,**

In Thy surrounding night to **roll,**

An atom past my own control,

In the unconscious sum **of Thee.**

VII.

APPREHENSION.

APPREHENSION.

I.

THE hills come down on every side,
  The marsh lies green below,
The green, green valley is long and wide,
Where the grass grows thick with the rush beside,
  And the white sheep come and go.

Down in the marsh it is green and still ;
  You may linger all the day,
Till **a** shadow slants from the western hill,
And the color goes out of the flowers in the rill,
  And the sheep look ghostly gray.

And never a change in the great green flat
  Till the change of night, my friend.
Oh wide green valley where we two sat,
How I longed that our lives were as peaceful as that,
  And seen from end to end !

II.

O foolish dream, to hope that such as I
  Who only answer to thine easiest moods,
  Should fill thy heart, as o'er my heart there broods
The perfect fulness of thy memory !
I flit across thy soul as white birds fly
  Across the untrodden desert solitudes :
  A moment's flash of wings ; fair interludes
That leave unchanged the eternal sand and sky.

Even such to thee am I ; but thou to me
As the embracing shore to the sobbing sea,
  Even as the sea itself to the stone-tossed rill.

But who, but who shall give such rest **to thee?**

The deep mid-ocean waters perpetually

   Call to the land, and call unanswered still.

III.

As dreams the fasting nun of Paradise,

   And finds her gnawing **hunger** pass away

   In thinking of the happy bridal day

That soon shall dawn upon her watching eyes,

So, dreaming of your love, do I despise

   Harshness or death of friends, doubt, slow decay,

   Madness, — all dreads **that** fill me with dismay,

And creep about me **oft with fell** surmise.

For you are true ; and **all** I hoped you **are ;**

   O perfect **answer** to my calling **heart !**

   And very sweet my life is, having thee.

Yet must I dread the dim end **shrouded** far ;

   Yet must I **dream :** should once **the good planks start,**

   How bottomless **yawns** beneath **the boiling sea !**

VIII.

LOVE AND VISION.

LOVE AND VISION.

My love is more than life **to me,**
　And you look on and wonder
In what can that enchantment be
　You think I labor under.

Yet you, too, have you never gone
　Some wet **and** yellow even
Where russet moors reach on and **on**
　Beneath a windy heaven? —

Brown moors which at the western edge
　A watery sunset brushes
With misty rays yon sullen ledge
　Of cloud casts down on the rushes.

You see no more ; but shade your eyes,
   Forget the showery weather,
Forget the wet, tempestuous skies,
   And look upon the heather.

Oh, fairyland, fairyland !
   It sparkles, lives, and dances,
By every gust swayed down and fanned,
   And every rain-drop glances.

Never in jewel or wine the light
   Burned like the purple heather ;
And some is the palest pink, some white,
   Swaying and dancing together.

Every stem is sharp and clear,
   Every bell is ringing,
No doubt, some tune we do not hear
   For the thrushes' sleepy singing.

Over all, like the bloom on a grape,
  The lilac seeding-grasses
Have made a haze, vague, without shape,
  For the wind to change as it passes.

Under all is the budding ling,
  Gray-green with scarlet notches,
Bossed with many a mossy thing,
  And gold with lichen-blotches.

Here and there slim rushes stand
  Aslant as carried lances.
I saw it and called it fairyland ;
  You never saw it, the chance is?

Brown moors and stormy skies that kiss
  At eve in rainy weather
You saw — but what the heather is
  Saw I, who love the heather.

IX

THE CONQUEST OF FAIRYLAND.

12

THE CONQUEST OF FAIRYLAND.

THERE reigned a king in the land of Persia, mighty and
    great was he grown,
On the necks of the kings of the conquered earth he
    builded up his throne.

There sate a king on the throne of Persia; and he was
    grown so proud
That all the life of the world was less to him than a
    passing cloud.

He reigned in glory: joy and sorrow lying between his
    hands.
If he sighed a nation shook, his smile ripened the harvest
    of lands.

He was the saddest man beneath the everlasting sky,

For all his glories had left him old, and the proudest
 king must die.

He who was even as God to all the nations of men,

Must die as the merest peasant dies, and turn into earth
 again.

And his life with the fear of death was bitter and sick
 and accursed,

As brackish water to drink of which is to be forever
 athirst.

The hateful years rolled on and on, but once it chanced
 at noon

The drowsy court was thrilled to gladness, it echoed so
 sweet a tune.

Low as the lapping of the sea, as the song of the lark is
 clear,

Wild as the moaning of pine branches ; the king was fain
 to hear.

" What is the song, and who **is** the singer?" he said;
    " before the throne
Let him come, **for** the songs of **the world** are mine, and
    all but this are **known."**

Seven mighty kings **went** out the minstrel man **to** find :
And all they found was a dead cypress soughing in **the**
    wind.

And slower still, and sadder still the heavy winters rolled,
And the burning summers waned away, and the king
    grew very old ;

Dull, worn, feeble, bent ; and once he thought, " To die
Were rest, at least." And as he thought the music wan-
    dered by.

Into the presence of the king, singing, the singer came,
And his face was like the spring in flower, his eyes were
    clear as flame.

"What is the song you play, and what the theme your
    praises sing?

It is sweet; I knew not I owned a thing so sweet," said
    the weary king.

"I sing my country," said the singer, "a land that is
    sweeter than song."

"Which of my kingdoms is your country?   Thither would
    I along."

"Great, O king, is thy power, and the earth a footstool
    for thy feet;

But my country is free, and my own country, and oh, my
    country is sweet!"

The eyes of the king, as he heard, grew young and alive
    with fire:

"Lo, is there left on the earth a thing to strive for, a
    thing to desire?

"Where is thy country? tell me, O singer! speak thine
  innermost heart!
Leave thy music! speak plainly! Speak — forget thine
  art!"

The eyes of the singer shone as he sang, and his **voice**
  rang wild and free
As the elemental wind or the uncontrollable sobs of the
  sea.

"O for my distant home!" he sighed; "Oh, alas! away
  and afar
I watch thee **now as a** lost sailor watches a shining
  star.

"Oh, that a wind would take me there! that a bird would
  set me down
Where the golden streets shine red at sunset in my
  father's town!

" For only in dreams I see the faces of the women
    there,

And fain would I hear them singing once, braiding their
    ropes of hair.

"Oh, I am thirsty, and long to drink of the river of Life,
    and I

Am fain to find my own country, where no man shall
    die."

Out of the light of the throne, the king looked down : as
    in the spring

The green leaves burst from their dusky buds, so was
    hope in the eyes of the king.

" Lo," he said, " I will make thee great ; I will make thee
    mighty in sway

Even as I ; but the name of thy country speak, and the
    place and the way."

" Oh, the way to my country is ever north till you **pass**
the mouth of hell,

Past the limbo **of** dreams and the desolate land where
shadows **dwell.**

" And when you have reached the **fount of wonder, you**
ford the waters **wan**

To the land of elves and the land of fairies, enchanted
Masinderan."

The singer ceased ; and the lyre in his hand snapped. as
a cord, in twain ;

And neither lyre nor singer was seen in the kingdom of
Persia again.

And all the nobles gazed astounded ; **no man spoke a
word**

Till the old king said : **" Call out my armies ;** bring me
hither a sword ! "

As a little torrent swollen by snows is turned to a terrible
  stream,

So the gathering voices of all his countries cried to the
  king in his dream.

Crying, " For thee, O our king, for thee, we had freely
  and willingly died,

Warriors, martyrs, what thou wilt; not that our lives
  betide

"The worth of a thought to the king, but rather, O ruler,
  because thy rod

Is over our heads as over thine is the changeless will of
  God.

" Rather for this we beseech thee, O master, for thine own
  sake refrain

From the blasphemous madness of pride, from the fever
  of impious gain."

" You **seek** my death," the king thundered ; " you cry,
 ' **Forbear** to save
The life of a king too old to frolic ; let him drowse in the
 grave.'

" **But I** will live for all your treason ; and, by my own
 right hand !
I will set out this day with you to conquer Fairy-
land."

Then all the nations paled aghast, for the battle to
 begin
Was a war with God, and a war with death, and they
 knew the thing was sin.

Sick at heart they gathered together, but none denounced
 the wrong,
For the will of God was unseen, unsaid, and the will of
 the king was strong.

So the air grew bright with spears, and the earth shook
    under the tread
Of the mighty horses harnessed for battle ; the standards
    flaunted red.

And the wind was loud with the blare of trumpets, and
    every house was void
Of the strength and stay of the house, and the peace of
    the land destroyed.

And the growing corn was trodden under the weight of
    armèd feet,
And every woman in Persia cursed the sound of a song
    too sweet,

Cursed the insensate longing for life in the heart of a sick
    old man ;
But the king of Persia with all his armies marched on
    Masinderan.

Many a day they marched in the sun till their silver
armor was **lead**

To sink **their bodies** into the grave, and many a man fell
dead.

And they passed the mouth of hell, and the shadowy
country gray,

Where the air is mist and the people mist and the rain
more real than they.

And they came to the fount of wonder, and forded the
waters **wan,**

And the king of Persia and **all** his armies marched on
Masinderan.

And they turned the rivers to blood, and the fields to a
ravaged camp,

Till they neared the golden faery town, that **burned in the**
dusk as **a lamp.**

And they stood and shouted for joy, to see it stand so
  nigh,
Given into their hands for spoil; and their hearts beat
  proud and high.

And the armies longed for the morrow, to conquer the
  shining town,
For there was no death in the land, neither any to strike
  them down.

And the hosts were many in numbers, mighty, and skilled
  in the strife,
And they lusted for gold and conquest as the old king
  lusted for life.

And, gazing on the golden place, night took them
  unaware,
And black and windy grew the skies, and black the
  eddying air —

So long the night and black the night that fell upon their
eyes,
They quaked with fear, those mighty hosts; the sun
would never rise.

Darkness and deafening sounds confused the black, tempestuous air,
And no man saw his neighbor's face, nor heard his neighbor's prayer.

And wild with terror the mad battalions fell on each other
in fight,
The ground was strewn with wounded men, mad in the
horrible night —

Mad with eternal pain, with darkness and stabbing
blows
Rained on all sides from invisible hands till the ground
was red as a rose.

And, though he were longing for rest, none ventured to
    pause from the strife,
Lest haply another wound be his to poison his hateful
    life.

And the king entreated death ; and for peace the armies
    prayed ;
But the gifts of God are everlasting, His word is not
    gainsaid.

Gold and battle are given the hosts, their boon is turned
    to a ban,
And the curse of the king is to live forever in conquered
    Masinderan.

SONG.

I HAVE lost my singing-voice ;
   My heyday 's over.
No more I lilt my cares and joys,
   But keep them under cover.
   My heyday 's gone :
   I sit and look on
While Life rushes past with a sob and a moan.

Wherefore should I stop to tell
   The pang that rends me ?
If it leave me all is well ;
   And if it last it ends me.
   Should one tear rise ·
   To my entrancèd eyes
It falls for a world full of hunger and sighs.

FAMOUS WOMEN SERIES.

—◆—

EMILY BRONTË.

By A. MARY F. ROBINSON.

One vol. 16mo. Cloth. Price, $1.00.

" Miss Robinson has written a fascinating biography. . . . Emily Brontë is interesting, not because she wrote 'Wuthering Heights,' but because of her brave, baffled, human life, so lonely, so full of pain, but with a great hope shining beyond all the darkness, and a passionate defiance in bearing more than the burdens that were laid upon her. The story of the three sisters is infinitely sad, but it is the ennobling sadness that belongs to large natures cramped and striving for freedom to heroic, almost desperate, work, with little or no result. The author of this intensely interesting, sympathetic, and eloquent biography, is a young lady and a poet, to whom a place is given in a recent anthology of living English poets, which is supposed to contain only the best poems of the best writers." — *Boston Daily Advertiser.*

" Miss Robinson had many excellent qualifications for the task she has performed in this little volume, among which may be named, an enthusiastic interest in her subject and a real sympathy with Emily Brontë's sad and heroic life. 'To represent her as she was,' says Miss Robinson, ' would be her noblest and most fitting monument.' . . . Emily Brontë here becomes well known to us and, in one sense, this should be praise enough for any biography." — *New York Times.*

" The biographer who finds such material before him as the lives and characters of the Brontë family need have no anxiety as to the interest of his work. Characters not only strong but so uniquely strong, genius so supreme, misfortunes so overwhelming, set in its scenery so forlornly picturesque, could not fail to attract all readers, if told even in the most prosaic language. When we add to this, that Miss Robinson has told their story *not* in prosaic language, but with a literary style exhibiting all the qualities essential to good biography, our readers will understand that this life of Emily Brontë is not only as interesting as a novel, but a great deal more interesting than most novels. As it presents most vividly a general picture of the family, there seems hardly a reason for giving it Emily's name alone, except perhaps for the masterly chapters on ' Wuthering Heights,' which the reader will find a grateful condensation of the best in that powerful but somewhat forbidding story. We know of no point in the Brontë history — their genius, their surroundings, their faults, their happiness, their misery, their love and friendships, their peculiarities, their power, their gentleness, their patience, their pride, — which Miss Robinson has not touched upon with conscientiousness and sympathy." — *The Critic.*

" ' Emily Brontë ' is the second of the ' Famous Women Series,' which Roberts Brothers, Boston, propose to publish, and of which ' George Eliot ' was the initial volume. Not the least remarkable of a very remarkable family, the personage whose life is here written, possesses a peculiar interest to all who are at all familiar with the sad and singular history of herself and her sister Charlotte. That the author, Miss A. Mary F. Robinson, has done her work with minute fidelity to facts as well as affectionate devotion to the subject of her sketch, is plainly to be seen all through the book." — *Washington Post.*

—————

Sold by all Booksellers, or mailed, post-paid, on receipt of price, by the Publishers,

ROBERTS BROTHERS, Boston.